A Mole Home

HAILEY SCRAGG • LISA PERRETT

What is in this hole?

POKE!
POKE!

Do not poke a nose
in this hole!

It is a home.

A hole home?

Is that a joke?

Do not have
that tone!

It is a mole home.

Take note.

Bug has a
log home.

Bat hangs in a
cave home.

13

Cub naps in a
den home.

Do NOT poke
that hole!

RUN!

hole	mole	poke
home	nose	tone
joke	note	

Decodable Words

bat	hang(s)	not
bug	in	run
cave	it	take
cub	log	
den	nap(s)	

High-Frequency Words

a	have	this
do	is	what
has	that	